A Word to Parents and Teachers . . .

COCO'S CANDY SHOP is a unique experience in Christian Education. The delights of childhood, popularized by such names as Seuss, Disney, and Sesame Street, are associated with joyous truths about God. This book does not seek to cover doctrines in depth, but to bring a happy association among the various facets of total living—serious and delightful, sacred and secular, truth and fantasy.

Read the book through at least once with your child before stopping to talk about the Bible truths. This will give him time to discover the delights of Coco and his friends without interruption. After your child becomes familiar with the story, he will be ready to discover with you the important truths about God. This will be especially rewarding if you help him associate some of his own experiences with each truth that is taught.

Printed in the United States of America

Coco's candy Shop

by V. Gilbert Beers
Illustrated by Marlene Short

THE SOUTHWESTERN COMPANY

Nashville, Tennessee

"Will you come? Will you come?"
shouted Kerry and Kay.
"Will you come with us now
on a trip for the day?
We will do many things
that are fun things to do,
but we want to do all
of these things now with you."

So then Coco the Bear
put his apron away
and he closed up his shop
for the rest of the day.
Then he filled up a bag
with some candy and things
while his friends all cried out,
"Look what Coco Bear brings!"

"Let us go! Let us go!"
said a rabbit called Zip.
"Let us go out right now
on this wonderful trip."
But the pig, who was Pudge,
only sat by the door
and he feasted on candy
while he asked for some more.

And poor Toto was tired
so he puffed when he ran,
while his friends went ahead
to the Bright Balloon Man.
"May we buy a balloon?"
all the happy friends said.
"It can be either blue,
or bright yellow or red."

"You may buy a balloon,
either yellow or blue,
or a special red one
that is made just for you.
You may have this balloon,"
said the Bright Balloon Man.
"Then please help me do this,
if you think that you can."

THE BALLOON PUZZLE:

While Coco and his friends buy the balloon that is made just for them, help the Balloon Man find what it says on his red balloons. This will tell you something about the way you are made.

"To the train!" shouted Zip,
as he ran on ahead.
"But please don't forget
what the red balloons said!"
Then the engineer came
with his engineer's suit,
and off they all went
with a puff and a toot.

"We are off to the farm,
on a very fine track,
with a huff and a puff
and a clickety clack.
I will guide you today,"
said the Engineer Man.
"But please help me do this,
if you think that you can."

God goes

THE TRAIN PUZZLE:

As the Engineer Man guides Coco and his friends on their trip, come along and do the train puzzle. It will tell you about Someone who guides you.

Happy Coco the Bear
gave a big candy cane
to the farmer who met
all the friends at the train.
"Here's a gumdrop for you
and a bon bon for me,
and some lollipops, too,
from the Lollipop Tree,"
said good Coco the Bear
to his friends. "While you rest,
you can eat all these things
which are better than best."

All the animals came
to say "how-do-you-do,"
and they brought some good gifts
for their friends to have, too.
The white goose gave some down,
a big pillow was full.
And the cow gave some milk,
while the sheep brought some wool.
"What good gifts you all give,"
shouted Kerry and Kay.
"We do thank you so much
that you helped us today."
"Now will you please help me,"
the kind Farmer began.
"Will you help me do this,
if you think that you can?"

THE FARM PUZZLE:

The Farmer wants you to read the sentences on his tractor tires. Which one is right, the one on the green tractor, or the one on the red tractor? What kind of gifts should you give to God? What should you say to God for His good gifts?

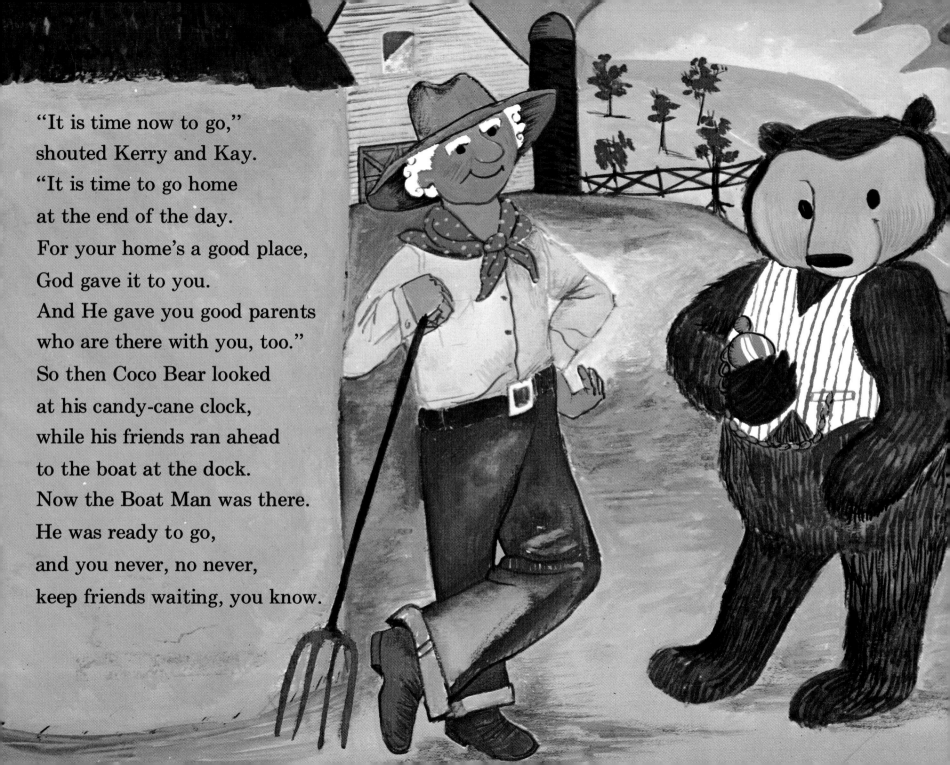

"It is time now to go,"
shouted Kerry and Kay.
"It is time to go home
at the end of the day.
For your home's a good place,
God gave it to you.
And He gave you good parents
who are there with you, too."
So then Coco Bear looked
at his candy-cane clock,
while his friends ran ahead
to the boat at the dock.
Now the Boat Man was there.
He was ready to go,
and you never, no never,
keep friends waiting, you know.

Then the boat started out,
it went out on the lake,
but a storm came along
and it made the boat shake.
The wind howled and it blew,
it blew over their heads,
and they all wished they were
safe at home in their beds.
"We must do something now,"
said the frightened Boat Man.
"Will you please tell me what
if you think that you can?"

THE BOAT PUZZLE:

Can you answer the Boat
Man? What do you do
when you need help? Look
at all the green letters in
the boat's name. They
will tell you what to do.
What do you tell God
when He helps you?

Then the storm stopped at last.
The boat came to the shore,
and they all were so glad
they had come home once more.
Now Pudge smiled as he looked.
He jumped up with a start,
as he saw on the street,
the Ice Cream Man's bright cart.

"Buy some ice cream for friends,"
said the man with the cart.
"It's a good way to show
all the love in your heart."
So Pudge bought some ice cream
for each friend who was there.
Then he said, "This will show
that I really do care."
"Now will you please help me?"
the Ice Cream Man began.
"Will you help me do this,
if you think that you can?"

THE ICE CREAM
PUZZLE:

God cares for someone
very much. He wants that
someone to love Him very
much, too. Do you know
who that someone is?
Look at the first letter of
each word in the special
flavor. They will tell you
who it is.

Special !!
Yummy
Orange
Upsicle

So at last the friends came
through the Candy Shop door,
Then Pudge feasted on candy
while he asked for some more.
But the day was too much,
for poor Toto, you see,
so he fell fast asleep
by the Lollipop Tree.
And good Coco the Bear
took his apron again,
and passed out some candy
to each happy friend.
"We thank you! We thank you!"
shouted Kerry and Kay.
"We are glad that you came
on our fun-filled day."
Are you glad you came along, too??